# Tiggy
## and the
# Lost Island

by Sheree Fulcher        Illustrated by Ismail Boujendar

This book is dedicated to my beautiful grandchildren:
Sunny, River, Hunter and Gaia.
Love you to the moon and back!

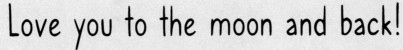

This book is independently published by Sheree Fulcher.


Written by copyrighted © Sheree Fulcher
Illustrated by copyrighted © Ismail Boujendar

ISBN:  979-8588383509

Tiggy looked out over the forest of eucalyptus trees. It was early and his friends were still asleep.

"What a beautiful morning," he said, "Far too good to be sleeping the day away."

He decided to go to the beach for a surf before breakfast.

Tiggy put on his favourite board shorts, grabbed his favourite surfboard, and wandered down to the beach.

The waves looked Perfect!

There were lots of other surfers out on the break.

He managed to catch several beautiful waves.

**Dude!   These waves were gnarly.**

He was having so much fun, he didn't realize the currents had changed.

The surf and swells grew **bigger** and there were lots of rips and strong currents.

Nearly all the other surfers had gone ashore already.

Tiggy decided to surf one more wave before heading in, too.

He was ready for a wave, but he was not ready for what happened next...

**Suddenly** a massive wave rose from the ocean and knocked him right off his board!

The rope that connected him to his board snapped and instantly, it was out of sight.

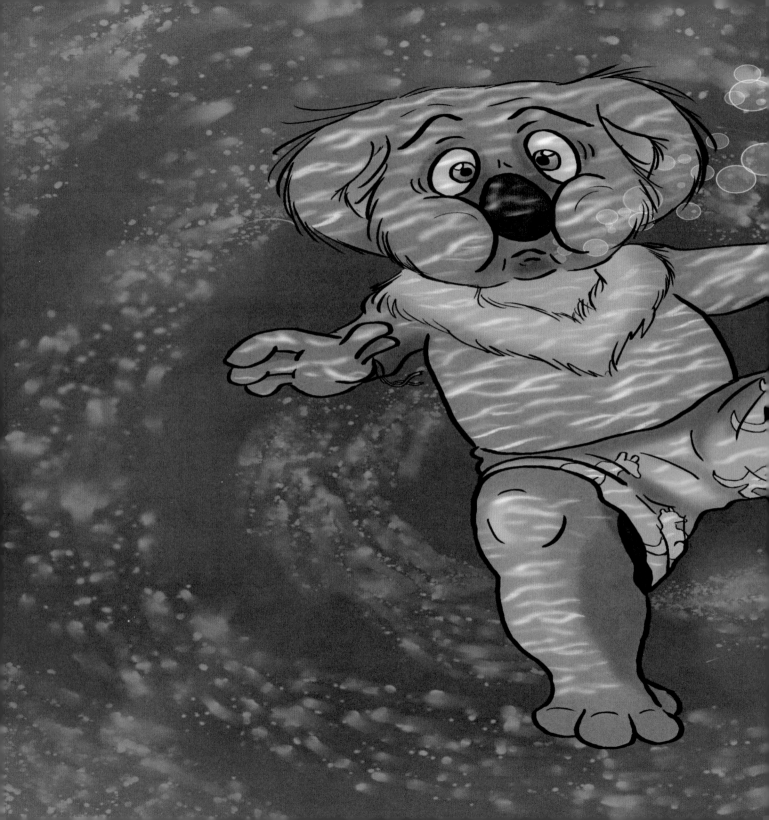

He swallowed a mouthful of water as he tried to find his way to the surface for air.

He flipped and tumbled in the wild spin of the water.

Then the fierce current pulled him underwater and dragged him along the ocean floor.

As Tiggy tumbled and spun, he grew dizzy, and more and more afraid.

**Would this wave ever let go?**

He started to think, and worry, that he might never make it back to the surface.

Just when Tiggy felt as though he couldn't breathe anymore, something grabbed hold of his hand.

Whatever-it-was, it pulled him into an underwater cave so he could get some air.

Tiggy coughed, gasped, and spat water, while trying to regain his bearings. He wondered where he was and what had happened.

He was confused, and a bit in shock. He looked around and saw a **monster, a unicorn, and a fairy.**

They stared at him....He stared back....

## Was he seeing things?

He shook his head, rubbed his eyes, and looked again. Sure enough....

**a monster, a unicorn, and a fairy.**

"I must be dreaming," he said.

"You're not dreaming, but you're alive!

# Hooray!

Are you okay?" they asked. "We thought you weren't going to make it," they said with tremendous concern.

Tiggy did not know where to begin asking questions but rambled what he wanted to know anyway,

**"Wait... what happened... and where am... and how, I mean, who are you?"**

The fairy explained, "I am Daisy Bell."
"This is Señorita Sparkle Hooves," she said, introducing her beautiful unicorn friend.

"And this is Fang" — he's a monster, but don't worry, he's totally friendly.

"What's your name?"
Tiggy introduced himself.

Then Daisy Bell continued, "And, to answer your question –

You are inside Golden Cave, on Rainbow Island, which is the most beautiful mystical island in the world."

"At least it used to be," said Señorita Sparkle Hooves rolling her eyes.

"What do you mean it used to be beautiful and mystical?" wondered Tiggy

"We'll explain everything. First, I'll make you a eucalyptus smoothie so you can recover quickly from your ordeal," said Daisy Bell.

That sounded great to Tiggy.

Once the energy smoothies were ready, they all sat down to share the story of Rainbow Island and how they ended up under the sea in Golden Cave.

Daisy Bell began, "Rainbow Island used to be invisible to the rest of the world – you know, people - and we lived in perfect peace and harmony.

All my fairy friends had unique little houses all over the island with special handmade decorations, and beautiful gardens.

We'd visit each other for smoothies or mini donuts. Everyone was welcoming and kind."

Tiggy said, "Sounds awesome!"

Señorita Sparkle Hooves described her experience on the island, "My friends and I had so much fun! There were hundreds of us, and we loved to gallop through fields of amazing flowers in every colour you could imagine. Everything was so pretty, and the gardens smelled so sweet! Sometimes we'd take the fairies for a ride and we'd scatter magic sparkles wherever we went."

Fang added, "And, my monster friends and I would wander the island doing silly things. We'd make everybody laugh with funny faces, jokes, and pranks. Nobody feared us. They thought we were very entertaining. We had so much fun together that we would laugh and laugh and laugh until we cried!"

"It was pure bliss," added Señorita Sparkle Hooves,    closing her eyes as she remembered those times fondly.

Daisy Bell interrupted the good memories,

## "Until one day" -

We don't know how they found us - but the pirate dogs came.

"Pirate dogs?" asked Tiggy.

"Yes," confirmed Daisy Bell. "Captain Rusty Sword, his first mate Sid-Bad-Breath, and their whole stinky crew.

They came on their big ship, the Wooden Kiel. They robbed us of all our prized possessions, and basically destroyed our houses, gardens, and parks.

## Everything!

They took all our home-grown, rainbow-colored fruits and vegetables, so we had nothing left to eat. They even took our special jewels."

"Jewels?" wondered Tiggy.

"I'll take it from here," said Señorita Sparkle Hooves,

"In the middle of the island, hidden in a statue, there were three jewels. The jewels are the source of the magic that kept Rainbow Island afloat and kept us invisible to people.

When they took the jewels, the magic faded, and Rainbow Island sunk to the bottom of the ocean. Our little island got caught in a rip, which pushed us into this cave. That's where we are right now."

"They destroyed Rainbow Island as we knew it. Down here in the cave, we don't get enough sunlight, so we can't grow the food we need to survive. I am afraid we will not last much longer," said Fang.

"That is terrible," gasped Tiggy. "So, where did everybody go?"

Daisy Bell said, "Well, some of the fairies thought it was too cold here, so they made homes in random gardens on the mainland. That way, they could enjoy the sun and warmth. And there would be plenty of food there, too."

Fang added, "The monsters went to live under the beds and in the closets of the children who live nearby. They were hoping to make friends with the children, but some of them were scared instead. This made the mums and dads upset, so they tried to chase the monsters away. We didn't want to scare them, we only wanted to make them laugh, like we used to do on Rainbow Island."

Señorita Sparkle Hooves put her hooves up in the air, "Unicorns need sun and space to run. Some of my friends left and I don't know where they ended up. I haven't seen them in forever. I miss them."

"So, why are you three still here?" wondered Tiggy.

"We can't bear to let Rainbow Island disappear forever," said Señorita Sparkle Hooves, "We want to save it and restore it to its former beauty and glory. Maybe then our friends will come back.

That would be soooo amazing!"

**"Can I help?" asked Tiggy. "YES! PLEASE!**

We need all the help we can get," said Daisy Bell.

"We heard that Captain Rusty Sword's boat capsized in a big storm. The crew dog-paddled ashore, but all their loot, including our jewels, sunk to the bottom of the ocean.

We know where the wreck is, and we can even see them sparkle, but we can't get to them. We can't swim or hold our breaths under water for that long.

Hey! You're a great surfer and swimmer – maybe you can dive down there and retrieve the jewels!"

The friends were beginning to feel a bit more hopeful about the future of Rainbow Island...

"Legend has it that once the jewels are back in place on the statue, the island will rise to the ocean's surface and will become invisible to people once again. Then all our friends can come back to the island, and we can live happily ever after!"

"I will help you. I will do my best," said Tiggy.

Early the next morning, the friends called on their mermaid friend, Oceania, to help Tiggy with the jewel rescue.

Oceania had helped them locate the jewels, but she was so tiny that she just couldn't lift or carry the jewels by herself. She needed help.

Oceania and Tiggy took off to recover the jewels.

Everything went smoothly... well, except for the fact that they were only able to find one jewel — the bright red one.

"They were here last time I was here. Someone must have taken them," suggested Oceania.

Oceania and Tiggy looked and looked around the whole underwater shipwrecked area, but they couldn't find the other two jewels.

"Oh well. Let's just head back," said Tiggy.

When they arrived back at Rainbow Island, everyone jumped for joy when they saw the bright jewels.

**"Thank you, thank you!" they shouted.**

"Wait... Where are the other two jewels?" Daisy Bell asked

the only one we could find... we looked everywhere near the ship, but there was no sign of the other two."

The excitement quickly faded from the friends' faces

"Do you think the pirate dogs took them?" wondered Fang.

"I wouldn't be surprised," said Señorita Sparkle Hooves.

"What do we do now?" said Daisy Bell sadly.

"Well, we don't give up – that's for sure!" said Tiggy. "We have to find the missing jewels wherever they are and get them back where they belong! Even if that means we've got to face those nasty pirate dogs!

And if the pirate dogs did take them, then we have to come up with a plan to outsmart them and get the jewels back."

Tiggy continued, "We must start looking right away, and we should ask everyone we know to help. We should send messages to all our friends and anyone who might have information that can help us.

As soon as we get the word out and pack up a few supplies, we should head out on our mission."

So, that's exactly what they did.

Made in the USA
Middletown, DE
02 May 2022